CARNY GAMES 3

A SEX PARTY

JADE'S EROTIC ADVENTURES
BOOK 51

VICTORIA RUSH

VOLUME 51

JADE'S EROTIC ADVENTURES - BOOK 51

COPYRIGHT

Carny Games 3 © 2022 Victoria Rush

Cover Design © 2022 PhotoMaras

All Rights Reserved

The Erotic Temple: A Sexy Fairytale (Coming Soon)

Erotica Themed Bundles:

Voyeur: Lesbian Erotica Bundle

Public Affairs: A Lesbian Anthology

Futa Fantasies: The Ladyboy Collection

Threesomes: The Lesbian Collection

Threesomes - Volume 2: The Lesbian Collection

First Time: A Lesbian Anthology

Hedonism: An Erotic Anthology

Switch Hitters: Bisexual Erotica

Taboo Erotica: The Lesbian Series

BDSM: The Lesbian Collection

Party Games: The Erotic Collection

Party Games 2: The Erotic Collection

All Girl 1: Lesbian Erotica Bundle

All Girl 2: Lesbian Erotica Bundle

All Girl 3: Lesbian Erotica Bundle

All Girl 4: Lesbian Erotica Bundle

Erotic Fairytale Bundles:

Clover's Fantasy Adventures: Books 1 - 5

Clover's Fantasy Adventures: Books 6 - 10

Erotic Fantasy:

Pirate's Bounty: A Time Travel Adventure

Wild West: A Time Travel Adventure

Private Riley: A Time Travel Adventure

Cleopatra's Secret: A Time Travel Adventure

Bounty Hunter 2125: A Time Travel Adventure

Ninja Assassin: A Time Travel Adventure

The 300: A Time Travel Adventure

Arabian Nights: An Erotic Fairytale (coming soon...)

Steamy Time Travel Bundles:

Riley's Time Travel Adventures: Books 1 - 5

Lesbian Erotica:

The Dinner Party: Lesbian Voyeur Erotica

The Darkroom: Bisexual Voyeur Erotica

Naked Yoga: Lesbian Transgender Erotica

Nude Cruise: Bisexual Voyeur Erotica

Rush Hour: Taboo Public Sex

The Girl Next Door: First Time Lesbian Erotic Romance

Girls' Camp: Lesbian Group Sex

Wet Dream: Ladyboy Fantasy Erotica

The Convent: Taboo Sex with a Nun

Sex Robot: A Dream Sex Machine

The Personal Trainer: Getting Pumped at the Gym

The Dominatrix: BDSM Lesbian Domination

Webcam Chat: Lesbian Online Sex

Paint Me: A Kinky Bodypainting Workshop

The Toy Party: Girls Sharing Sex Toys

The Costume Party: Strapping One On

Swedish Sauna: Lesbian Group Sex

The Therapist: Taboo Lesbian Erotica

Elevator Shaft: Bisexual Threesomes Erotica

Ladyboy: Lesbian Transgender Erotica

Peep Show: Lesbian Voyeur Erotica

The Dare: Public Sex Erotica

Maid Service: Lesbian Threesomes Erotica

The Hitchhiker: First Time Lesbian Erotica

The Housesitter: Spycam Lesbian Erotica

The Spa: Lesbian Group Orgy

Parlor Games: Blindfold Sex Party

The Exchange Student: First Time Lesbian Erotica

The Hostel: Bisexual Group Erotica

The Harem: Lesbian Erotic Romance

The Orient Express: Lesbian Voyeur Erotica

The First Lady: A Forbidden Lesbian Erotic Romance

The Slave: Lesbian BDSM Erotica

The Masseuse: Lesbian Sensuous Erotica

Too Close for Comfort: Lesbian Forbidden Erotica

Naked Twister: A Wild Party Game

Lexi: The Sex App (Lesbian Fantasy Erotica)

Call Girl: Lesbian Bisexual Threesomes Erotica

Circle Jill: Lesbian Masturbation Workshop

The Viewing Room: Masturbation Voyeur Erotica

Spin the Bottle: A Kinky Party Game

The Hair Salon: Lesbian Voyeur Erotica

Tribadism 1: Girls Only Sex Workshop

Tribadism 2: The Art of Scissoring

Tribadism 3: Threeway Hookups

The Kiss: A Game of Oral Sex

Pledge Week: Sorority Sisters

Carny Games 1: A Wild Sex Party

Carny Games 2: A Kinky Sex Party

Carny Games 3: An Erotic Sex Party

Dreamscape: An Artificial Reality Game

Glory Hole: Guess Who's On the Other Side

Joy Ride: A Late Night Erotic Bus Trip

The Blind Girl: An Erotic Romance(Coming Soon)

Lesbian Erotica Bundles:

Jade's Erotic Adventures: Books 1 - 5

Jade's Erotic Adventures: Books 6 - 10

Jade's Erotic Adventures: Books 11 - 15

Jade's Erotic Adventures: Books 16 - 20

Jade's Erotic Adventures: Books 21 - 25

Jade's Erotic Adventures: Books 26 - 30

Jade's Erotic Adventures: Books 31 - 35

Jade's Erotic Adventures: Books 36 - 40

Jade's Erotic Adventures: Books 41 - 45

Jade's Erotic Adventures: Books 46 - 50

Fifty Shades of Jade: Superbundle

Standalone Stories:

The Polynesian Girl: A Lesbian EroticRomance

For the uninhibited...

WANT TO AMP UP YOUR SEX LIFE?

Sign up for my newsletter to receive more free books and other steamy stuff. Discover a hundred different ways to wet your whistle!

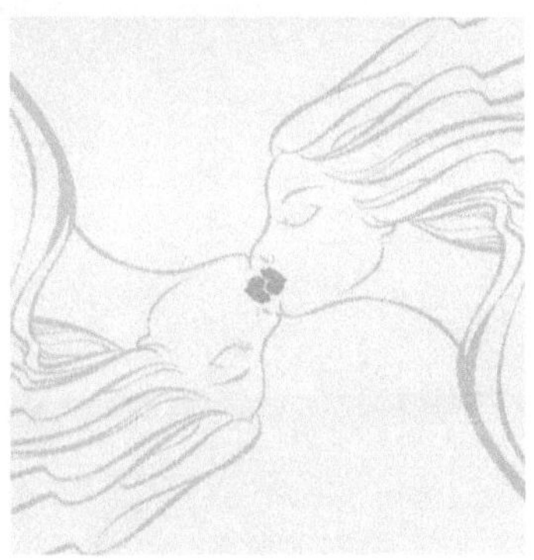

Victoria Rush Erotica

1

Two weeks after her first carnival-themed sex party, I received another email message from Madison, inviting me to her next event. The subject heading read *Carny Games 2*, and I almost tripped over my office chair rushing to open the message on my computer.

Dear Jade,

You are cordially invited to another party at my place this Saturday evening starting at 9 p.m.

The theme once again will be carnival games, where everyone will participate in more erotic contests simulating county fair games.

With names like Firing Range, Paint by Numbers, Bobbing for Peaches, and Orgasm Face, these games will make you laugh and squeal in equal measure.

But these contests aren't for the faint of heart, so be prepared to take your clothes off and let it all hang out. And remember to park your inhibitions at the door, because there's no telling who you'll be paired up with. From boy-on-girl to girl-on-girl to boy-on-boy to other surprise pairings, you can be sure to stretch your imagination in more ways than one.

So come clean, come prepared, and come often. Because we're going to have a ribald and riotous good time!

RSVP before Thursday,

Maddy

P.S.: Please bring an ink blot of your pussy to be used for a special game of Guess the Rorschach. The easiest way to do this is to spread food coloring on your vulva then sit with your legs apart on a clean sheet of paper under your ass.

WTF? I thought, after reading her message. *Guess the Rorschach? Paint by Numbers? Orgasm Face? This girl really does have too much time on her hands.*

Nonetheless, the idea of participating in another one of her kinky parties with some of my friends and a few new strangers was getting me incredibly turned on. I slipped my hand under my panties and thrust two fingers into my pussy, caressing myself while I imagined what she'd dreamed up this time.

WHEN I ARRIVED at Madison's house on the night of the party, she collected my pussy pictures, then escorted me to the living room where I saw many of my friends from her last party lounging around, sipping wine. But there were also a few *new* faces in the crowd, and as I scanned the tight figures of the participants, my panties began to moisten.

Brad and Laura had returned, plus there was a *new* married couple, Toby and Elle, looking like movie stars straight out of the pages of People Magazine. I nodded toward my friends Lily, Bonnie, and Emma from my last camping trip, and smiled at my friends from work, Ryan, Marco, and Neil. I was happy to see the cute Hispanic hunk Diego was back, as was the hung African-American dreamboat, Lincoln. And of course, no sex party would be complete without the participation of my sexy transgendered friend, Shae.

But I was surprised to see two familiar participants from my Fountain of Venus squirting workshop, the pretty African-American goddess Trinity, and the cute redhead, Piper. While my eyes darted around the room and I began to mingle with the group, I suddenly became conscious of the growing wet spot in the crotch of my jeans. After a few minutes, Trinity brushed up beside me and grinned, caressing the back of my ass.

"I see you haven't lost your special talent developed at our last workshop," she said, slipping her finger between my cheeks.

"And I haven't even *come* yet," I grunted, squirming in response to her touch. "But if you keep doing that, I'm *really* going to make a mess of myself."

"Mmm," she smiled. "I can't wait. What's this party all about? When I saw Madison's invitation, I was perplexed by the names of the games."

"That makes *two* of us," I said, twisting my hips away from her probing hand. "If it's anything like the last one, I won't be the *only* one squirting before long. She always comes up with the wildest party ideas."

"Did you bring your pussy blots?"

"Yes," I nodded. "It was kind of weird making them, but when I saw the final result, I thought it looked quite interesting. Mine reminds me of a lotus flower, how about yours?"

"Mine looks more like a bat with flapping wings," Trinity

chuckled. "I'm not quite sure what she intends to do with these pictures, but my pussy is already throbbing watching some of these hot party guests."

"You have no idea," I smiled, nodding toward Lincoln and Shae. "Lincoln's hung like a horse, and that pretty girl has got a prick you wouldn't believe."

"She's a *tranny*?" Trinity said, flaring her eyes while she stared at Shae. "I never would have guessed."

"Technically, she's a hermaphrodite," I said. "A rare individual with both male and female sex organs. She's quite versatile and enjoys mixing it up with *women* as much as men. But don't call her a tranny, she prefers to be referred to as a ladyboy. Would you like me to introduce you?"

"Yes, please," Trinity said, licking her lips.

But just as the two women began chatting, Madison called the meeting to order, and a hush fell over the room, with everybody excited to begin the festivities.

2

———

"Has everybody helped themselves to some wine and refreshments in the kitchen?" she said, nodding toward the gleaming island bedecked with cheese tarts, cucumber canapés, and crab cakes.

When everybody nodded and raised their glasses filled with Rioja and Chardonnay, she smiled, moving in front of the fireplace to address the group.

"I see a lot of familiar faces as well as a few new ones. For those of you not familiar with the theme of this party, everybody will be participating in a series of contests patterned after carnival games."

"Will there be prizes for the winners, like in the county fair?" Trinity said.

"There'll be prizes alright," Maddy grinned. "But they're going to be a little warmer and softer than the ones you might be used to."

"And *wetter*," Laura joked.

"Or *harder*, depending on which side of the contest wins," her husband Brad said.

"Yes," Madison nodded. "The carnival games in this party

are going to be a little more risqué and provocative than the ones at your typical county fair."

The new married couple shifted their weight uneasily, gripping each other's hands tightly.

"Will we be performing these fully *clothed*?" Elle said, glancing at her husband nervously.

"I suppose you could perform *some* of them that way," Maddy chuckled. "But I think you'll find most are a lot more fun experienced naked."

"And we'll be performing most of these games in *pairs*?" Elle's husband said.

"Most of them, yes," Madison said. "Though the couplings will be fairly random, so I hope you came prepared to mix it up. Variety is the spice of life, and this venue will offer plenty of opportunity for mixed-gender hookups."

Toby and Elle peered at one another for a long moment, then they nodded softly.

"So, what's our *first* challenge?" Shae said, stepping forward a few paces. "I wasn't sure if you wanted a picture of *my* pussy too, since I've got a bit of an unusual arrangement down there."

"Absolutely," Maddy smiled, pulling the prints of the women's pussies out of a folder and taping them up against the fireplace mantel. "Anyone with a vulva is free to partici-pate in this game. In fact, I think we should all take a moment to celebrate the magnificent diversity of this female feature. Take a look at these pictures, and revel in the sublime beauty of our sexual organs."

Everybody stepped forward a few feet, taking turns peering at the lineup of colorful imprints, each outlined in a different shape like a panel of expressionist paintings.

"Wow," Piper said, leaning in to examine some of the

prints. "And here I was so self-conscious of my own flappy folds. Each of these vulvas is quite unique and different, like the flowers of an English garden."

"Exactly," Madison nodded. "I think Georgia O'Keeffe captured it perfectly with her exotic renderings of sensuous blossoms. Each one so soft and delicate, like the women they belong to."

"Are these what we're going to be using for the *Guess the Rorschach* contest?" Laura said.

"Yes," Maddy said. "Each of the men will be given a random ink blot, then they'll have to guess which woman it belongs to."

"By lining up next to one another *naked*?" Elle said, widening her eyes.

"Like I said," Madison grinned. "It's a lot more fun playing these games naked."

"Talk about *variety*," Toby said, squinting at the colorful inkblots one at a time. "If Rorschach was right about our interpretations of these paintings reflecting our inner thoughts, we could have a *field day* comparing the pictures."

"This one looks like a chimpanzee riding a bicycle, Brad laughed, pressing his face close to one of the pictures. "What does that say about me?"

"That you're a pervert who likes to stare at women's pussies?" his wife Laura frowned.

"Well, pretty soon he's going to have a chance to get even closer than he imagined," Madison chuckled. "Because in this next game, the women will be lining up to display their *real* vulvas while the men attempt to match the pictures to the artists."

"What will be the prize for the winner?" Diego said.

"As with my previous party, the men who match the correct paintings to their owners will get the opportunity to examine their pussies with more than just their *eyes*. Subject to their partner's approval, of course."

"And each of the pairings will be randomly assigned?" Neil said.

"Of course," Madison grinned. "It's a *party* after all. Isn't the purpose of every party to mingle and have fun getting to know one another?"

"Not in the *biblical* sense," Bonnie joked.

"Nobody's forcing anyone to hook up with anybody they don't want to," Madison said. "But if this unfolds in any way similar to the last time, it won't take long for everybody to lose their inhibitions. Are you ready to get started?"

The party guests peered at one another, then each of them nodded slowly. I glanced around the room, noticing some of the men's crotches bulging in anticipation, with an equal number of the women's jeans darkening between their thighs. Apparently, more of them were excited about getting started with the contest than they were letting on.

Madison pulled the pictures down from the fireplace and handed one copy to each of the men, then she instructed the women to take off their clothes and relax on the sectional sofa, sitting side-by-side.

"Do you want us to take *everything* off?" Piper asked.

"Technically," Madison said. "You only need your *lower half* exposed. But if you feel comfortable, feel free to let it all hang out. I expect everybody will be getting fully naked soon enough, so you might as well get used to it at your first opportunity."

"What about the *men*?" Diego smiled.

"There's not much advantage in *your* being naked at this point," Madison laughed. "But don't worry–your turn will come soon enough in the next round I'm calling *Firing Range*."

"I can't wait to see what *that* involves," Ryan laughed, glancing at the image he'd been given and peering toward Shae with a familiar grin.

"Do we just hand our pictures to our counterparts once we've made a decision?" Lincoln asked.

"That'll work," Maddy nodded. "Once everyone's finished, I'll match the codes on the back with the correct owners."

"Then the fun will *really* begin," Brad smiled.

"Just try to keep your dick in your pants until we're *finished*," Laura huffed. "At least leave some of the spoils for the rest of the group."

"It's going to be difficult," Brad grinned, rearranging his hardening tool. "This thing has a mind of its own."

3

―――――――

After the women removed their clothes and sat on the sofa, each of the men lined up single file, crawling on their hands and knees to compare the picture they'd been given with each of the women's vulvas. While the women spread their legs and proudly displayed their pussies, the men glanced back and forth, squinting their eyes as they shook their heads uncertainly. Some of them took longer than others to examine the women's crotches, and when Brad paused for a long moment to stare at Trinity's pussy, Laura glanced up at Madison with an annoyed expression.

"Isn't there a *timer* on this game?" she said. Because if we let my husband have his way, this contest will *never* be over!"

"I didn't think it would be necessary," Madison chuckled. "But now that you mention it, why don't we limit each man to ten seconds per participant. I thought you boys were eager to get to the fun part?"

"This *is* the fun part," Brad grinned, straightening out his erection. "Talk about foreplay. I haven't been this turned on since I peeked at my first Penthouse magazine."

"If you don't move along smartly, you'll have to pull out your old collection when we get home," Laura huffed. "Because that's the only pussy you'll be seeing for a while if you deny the rest of the men a chance to finish this contest."

As the men continued down the line, I became more and more excited watching them staring at my throbbing pussy while my juices dripped down my legs. When Lincoln finally pulled up next to me, I glanced at the picture in his hand and nodded softly.

"We never got a chance to hook up at Madison's last party," I smiled. "But I would have thought you've seen enough of my pussy by now to recognize the familiar signs."

"Mmm," he nodded, peering back and forth between me and the blot of my pussy, before handing me the image gently. "I'm looking forward to pollinating your flower when everybody finishes this exercise. Save that thought, and I'll be back soon enough."

After all the men finished inspecting the women's vulvas and handed their pictures to their chosen candidates, Madison walked down the line, turning over each of the women's pictures to cross-reference the codes on the back with the notes she'd made on her clipboard.

"That was harder than it looked," Marco sighed. "Some of those Rorschach blots are just as mysterious as the owners they belong to."

"That's the idea," Maddy said, placing an X or a check mark on the back of each picture before handing them back to the women. "We wouldn't want to make it too easy for you. Just like at the country fair, you've got to *work* to win your prize."

"I actually found the images highly *erotic*," Ryan said, winking at Shae with a lopsided grin. "The impressions of their *anuses* were almost as vivid as those of their vulvas."

"Not to mention their *clitorises*," Diego nodded. "Are you sure we can't take some of these pictures back with us as a memento of our participation in the event?"

"I suppose that'll be up to your *partners*," Madison smiled. "Depending on how well you do in the next phase of this contest. Ladies, are you ready to reveal your scores?"

The women turned over their prints and glanced at Maddy's notes, then some of us peered up with broad smiles on our faces.

"It looks like Lincoln guessed *me* right," I said, flipping my page around to show Madison's check mark.

Then Shae turned her image around, glancing in the direction of Ryan.

"And Ryan guessed me also," she nodded. "Although I think he had a bit of an unfair advantage with my hard *cock* in place of the usual clitoris."

Suddenly, Elle shifted uncomfortably on the sofa, darting her eyes nervously in her husband's direction.

"And *Diego* guessed me right too," she said, turning her picture around slowly.

"So what happens now?" Toby said, crossing his arms over his chest.

"That depends on the women," Madison nodded. "We said the winners would have a chance to hook up with their partners. How they choose to do that exactly depends on how their counterparts wish to engage."

"Well, I don't know about *you* girls," I grinned, staring at Lincoln's python snaking down the leg of his pants. "But I've been looking forward to riding Lincoln's beanstalk ever since the last party."

Elle paused while she slowly ran her eyes up and down Diego's taut body.

"I'm not quite ready to jump into full-on coupling right

out of the gate," she said. "Maybe we could ease into this a little more slowly..."

"You seemed to enjoy having my face close to your vulva while I was examining you," Diego smiled. "Perhaps I can pay homage to your pretty pussy with a *different* part of my anatomy?"

Then he glanced over in Toby's direction.

"Assuming you two are willing to share the spoils?"

Toby hesitated for a moment, then he nodded slowly.

"We didn't come to this party to be prudes," he said. "We knew what we were getting ourselves into when we accepted the invitation. I'm game if my wife is."

Diego peered back at Elle, and she nodded softly as her mouth curled slowly upward.

"Speaking of different *parts*," Ryan said, glancing between Shae's legs at her upturned erection. "I'd love to lick you somewhere *else* if you're up for it. We gay men have learned that the anus can be just as sensitive as the other parts of the perineum. I'd love to jerk your pretty pole while I caress your *pucker*, if you're willing."

"Oh, I'm willing, alright," Shae grinned, dripping a drop of pre-cum over her flaring glans while she imagined the treat she was about to receive.

4

———

The three men knelt in front of their partners then they one by one lowered their heads between the women's legs, humming softly while they teased and sucked their folds. Shae was the first one to gasp out loud when she felt Ryan's tongue on her sphincter, grabbing her throbbing cock with two hands while he teased her rosebud. Elle was the next one to utter a groan, as she closed her eyes and surrendered to Diego's expert manipulation of her hardening clit with his flickering tongue.

While I stared at Lincoln's bobbing head between my knees, becoming increasingly turned on by his gentle caressing of my labia, I was tempted to lift his head off my pussy and pull him closer to my dripping hole, eager to feel his thick organ inside me. As I reveled in the sight of the other women moaning and sighing beside me, I felt my pleasure slowly building while he teased and caressed me.

"Jesus," I grunted, watching his face eating my pussy. "Who knew you were as good with your *tongue* as your big prick? If you keep doing that to me, you're going to make me come even before I feel you inside me."

"I'm not sure about the *rules*," Lincoln smiled, lifting his head to peer at me with dripping lips. "But if we're only allowed one orgasm per partner, we better get busy before we run out of time. How would you like me to give it to you?"

"If you're referring to what *position*," I grinned. "I'll take it any way I can get it. But I kind of like you on your knees. Why don't you fuck me from the front while I watch your beautiful instrument going in and out of me?"

"Mmm," Lincoln nodded. "I like the sound of that. Plus, you'll be able to control how much of me you take inside. In certain other positions, I'm liable to hurt you."

When he leaned back, I noticed his English-cucumber-sized dick flapping up in front of him.

"Just go slow while I savor every inch of you," I smiled, feeling my pussy beginning to leak like a faucet.

He pressed his hips forward, and I grasped the head of his instrument, pointing it toward my hole. When he slipped it inside my slit, I gasped feeling him spreading me apart, then I pushed my hips forward a few inches to take more of him inside me.

"God, yes," I grunted, watching his thick pole disappearing inside my pussy while he rocked his hips forward and back. "What a beautiful sight this is. I just want to *watch* you while you fuck me."

"Your *pussy* is beautiful, too," he moaned, watching my lips flaring around his shaft while my nub slid along the top of his veiny shaft. "I knew it was yours as soon as I saw you."

"You mean you didn't need my help matching the picture after all?"

"No," he grinned. "I've had the image of your pussy seared into my memory ever since the *Matching the Curtains with the Carpet* contest from our first party."

"I had no idea," I grunted, placing my hands on his hard

pecs and drifting them down over his washboard stomach. "All this time I thought you barely *noticed* me while you were busy fucking the other women."

"I noticed, alright," he huffed, a soft flush beginning to form on his chest and beginning to spread up his neck. "I was just biding my time, waiting for a chance to win one of the games with you."

"Well, it was worth the wait," I panted, lowering my fingers onto his throbbing cock and gripping it with both hands while he pounded me with the upper half. "This is the most magnificent tool I've ever seen. I'm just afraid you'll blow me apart when you climax. I remember how much you shoot when you come."

"Almost as much as *you* do if I remember correctly," Lincoln grinned, grabbing the sides of my ass and pulling me harder over his flexing organ. "I think we're a good match in more ways than one."

"Yes," I growled. "I want to feel you explode inside me while I watch you pulsing in my hands. This is the sexiest thing I've done in ages."

"I got the impression you preferred *women* from our last experience?" Lincoln rasped, growing closer to the tipping point.

"Sometimes," I nodded, squeezing his dick harder in my hands. "But I haven't had a dildo as big and hard as *this* one to play with for quite some time now."

"You're going to make me come if you keep squeezing me like that," he hissed.

"Oh yeah?" I grinned. "Do you like that? Open the taps on this firehose. I can feel you pulsing already."

"Yes," Lincoln moaned, his pupils rapidly dilating while he stared into my eyes. "I'm going to come, babe. Feel me when I come, oh God–"

Suddenly, he growled like a wild animal as I felt his thick tool pulsing in my hands. Normally, I didn't feel it when a man came inside me, but in this case the jetting of his hard squirts against my cervix only added to my excitement, and when I saw him climaxing, I quickly lost control over my own pleasure, and as he spasmed against my rolling hips, I began squirting hard over his balls.

"Oh *fuckkk*," he groaned, peering down to watch me spurting along with him while I held his cock tightly, daring him to try pulling out of me.

While our simultaneous orgasm seemed to go on forever, I peered over at Elle and Shae, who soon after also started climaxing as Diego and Ryan sucked their pussies. While the three of us shuddered in mutual ecstasy, I glanced at the rest of the group, who were looking on with their mouths agape and crotches dripping. Even Elle's husband was rubbing his bulging hard-on as he gazed into his wife's glassy eyes.

I don't imagine they'll be keeping their clothes on much longer, I grinned. *If I know Maddy, she's already planning the next event to raise the bar even higher.*

5

____

After the three of us recovered from our orgasms, the men seemed particularly eager to get started with the next contest, remembering how Madison usually alternated between the boys and the girls. Ryan and Diego seemed especially excited, with their erect penises clearly visible in the outline of their pants.

"Mmm," Maddy grinned, glancing toward our still-dripping pussies. "Are you guys hungry for a little more?"

"More _pussy_?" Brad said, turning toward Madison with raised eyebrows. "I thought it was the _boys'_ turn for a little excitement this time?"

"Right you are, Brad," Madison smiled. "In our next game I'm calling _Paint by Numbers_, you're going to have a chance to dip your quill in a slightly different manner. After all, you could use some practice using your dicks to stimulate us in some manner other than pounding it in and out of our pussies, am I right, ladies?"

"Damn straight, Maddy," Laura nodded.

"Well, in this _next_ contest, they're going to have a chance to use their instruments more creatively, by painting a picture for each of us."

"With our *penises*?" Marco said, bulging his eyes.

"Of course," Maddy said. "What fun would it be if you did it the usual way?"

"What will we be using for pigment?" Neil said.

Madison reached into her party kit and pulled out eight bowls of colorful cream, placing each bowl on separate tables scattered around the room.

"This paint is actually a type of food dye that I've created specially for the occasion," Maddy smiled. "It's body-safe and non-allergenic, and feels quite sensuous to the touch, not unlike certain types of lube."

"It looks like it'll be the *boys'* turn to smear food coloring all over their genitals this time," Emma grinned, nodding at the other women.

"Exactly," Madison said. "Except in this case, it will be a slightly more *active* exercise."

"What will we be using as our canvas?" Lincoln said. "Unless you want us to smear the paint on the walls like children?"

"It's going to be a big enough clean-up operation as it is," Madison chuckled, reaching behind the sectional sofa to lift a stack of small cardboard easels. "Can you ladies help me set these up next to each of the bowls? You'll see the instructions on the back of each panel."

Shae paused for a moment while she counted the bowls, then she peered back at Madison.

"I'm assuming because there's eight bowls and only seven guys that you'd like me to join the *men's* side this time?" she said.

"Absolutely," Maddy smiled. "Anyone equipped with a penis is eligible to participate in this contest. That is, assuming you're able to still get it up after your rimming by Ryan in the last contest. It'll be a little difficult to perform this exercise with a floppy dick."

"I think I can manage that," Shae nodded, caressing her thickening organ with her right hand.

Toby squinted at the bowls of paint then he peered toward Madison with a raised eyebrow.

"Is there a reason why we're using *food dye* instead of the usual body paint?" he said.

"I'm glad you asked, Toby," Madison said. "Because the winner of this contest will have a randomly selected participant *lick* it off their dicks when they're finished."

Toby glanced toward his wife, and she cocked her head with a lopsided smile.

"Looks like it might be *your* turn to mix it up this time, baby," she said.

"With any luck," Toby grinned.

"How will we decide who's the winner of the contest?" Diego asked.

"The women will be asked to vote on the most interesting composition."

"Will we be judged on *creativity or accuracy*?" Lincoln said.

"Both," Maddy smiled. "You've heard the expression that a good dancer is also a good lover? Let's see if the same can be said about *painters*."

"Don't worry, Linc," I said. "I'll let you paint on *my* canvas any time you want."

"Will this be a *timed* contest?" Ryan asked.

"As much as I don't want to rush you guys learning how to use your instruments more creatively, I'm afraid we're going to have to," Madison nodded. "We still have quite a few games to follow after this, and you're going to need to conserve your energy for some of the more difficult ones. Ten minutes should be more than enough time."

"I can't imagine what could be more difficult than painting a picture with our *dicks*," Lincoln chuckled.

"Don't worry, I've got some good ones lined up," Madison said, peering down at the men's bulging trousers. "Are you guys ready to get started? Because it's going to be pretty hard to perform this game with your *pants* on."

When the men took off their trousers, their hard-ons quickly sprung to life, revealing how excited they were at the idea of the women watching them paint with their cocks.

"Mmm," Laura grinned, licking her lips. "That's the most delicious sight I've seen in a long time. I'm ready to lick those dicks even before they get started."

"At least you can wait until everyone's seated at the table," Brad joked, echoing her comment from the last round. "Try to save a little bit for the *rest* of the women."

6

Each of the men took a position in front of one of the bowls, then they dipped their erections in the colorful cream and began swiping the tips across the paper easels. I found it interesting that Madison had made a different food color for each bowl, and as the men began to slap their dicks awkwardly against the easels, their meandering patterns started off looking more like toddlers' random finger painting than any kind of recognizable portrait. But after a couple of minutes, some of their illustrations began to take shape, reflecting familiar patterns and symbols.

Marco started off creating a simple smiley face with two dots and a curved line for the mouth, but after the women chided him for his lack of creativity, he tried to embellish his figure with a wavy stick figure.

"Come on, Marco," Lily laughed. "You're going to have to do better than that if you expect one of us to put a happy face on *you* when this contest is over. I hope your lovemaking isn't as one-dimensional as your draughtsmanship."

"It's a lot harder than it looks," he huffed, swiveling his

hips from side to side as he tried to control the direction of his blue-paint-coated penis over the paper. "I'm not used to using my penis this way."

"Well, you better get *used* to it," Bonnie chuckled. "Because nobody likes a lover who does it the same boring way every time."

"At least *Neil* chose a more inspiring subject," Emma nodded, turning toward the next easel.

He'd chosen to paint a heart with his red food color, with three radiating outlines symbolizing a beating organ.

"True," I nodded. "But it's not exactly a *Rembrandt*. "Can't you guys try to paint something a little more three-dimensional?"

"It's pretty obvious where *Ryan's* mind is going," Laura nodded, glancing at Ryan's rendering of a woman's ass with a set of balls nestled under her cheeks.

"What can I say?" Ryan grinned, tilting his orange-hued dick higher up the easel to outline his subject's back with two breasts peeking out the sides. "I seem to be developing an affinity for *ladyboys*."

"Unlike *Brad*," Trinity chuckled, peering at Brad's easel. "He seems to have a one-track mind."

He'd chosen to paint a crude rendition of the trucker's mudflap girl, showing a yellow silhouette of a naked women sitting with her arms outstretched behind her.

"Seriously?" Laura huffed, glaring at Brad. "Is that the only way you think of women? Like sexualized *bimbos*?"

"Well, it's not like Madison's *helping* anything with this erotic-themed party," Brad grunted. "With everyone taking off their clothes and getting freaky in increasingly kinky games, it's pretty hard to think of anything else."

"At least *Diego's* chosen to represent his appreciation for women in a more subtle way," Laura said, turning her head toward Diego's canvas.

His painting showed a flower with soft pink petals and a protruding pistil, echoing the image of a woman's vulva and clitoris.

"Does that remind you of anyone in *particular*?" I said, smiling in Elle's direction.

"Maybe," Diego nodded. "But *every* woman's flower is a work of art."

"Ohhh," Elle sighed, glancing at the other girls with swooning eyes. "That's the nicest thing anyone's ever said to me."

"Did you hear that, Toby?" Laura said, turning her head toward Elle's husband's easel. "It looks like you've got a little catching up to do with the front-runner."

"I'm trying my best," Toby said, twisting his hips while he painted an elaborate landscape scene on his easel.

When everybody turned to glance at his drawing, they gasped in surprise when they saw what he'd produced. His illustration showed a leafy tree at the side of lake with two green butterflies dancing next to one another.

"Holy cow," Piper said. "I think you may have missed your calling, Toby. If you're as adept with that brush in the *bedroom* as you are in front of an easel, your wife must be one lucky girl."

"I might have to watch him do this more often," Elle nodded, rubbing her thighs together while she gazed at her husband's dripping phallus. "This is the best foreplay I've ever had."

"That leaves only two more candidates to consider," Trinity nodded, twisting her head to the last couple of easels.

Everybody turned toward *Shae's* easel, where she'd

drawn a gender pictogram combining both the male and female symbols.

"I like it," Piper said. "They say everyone's sexual preference is somewhere on the continuum. I think we should *all* adopt this symbol to reflect our orientation."

Then everyone's eyes turned toward Lincoln, whose buttocks were flexing rapidly while he attempted to etch something on his board. We twisted our bodies to see what he was drawing, and our eyes widened when we saw what he'd produced. In near-perfect italic script, he'd written the words *love is the answer*.

"Oh my God," Emma gasped, flaring her eyes at the composition. "How can anyone write that clearly with their *penis*? I haven't been able to write in cursive since elementary school."

"It's pretty impressive," I nodded. "Especially considering the *thickness* of his brush."

"One minute left," Madison announced, glancing at her timer. "You guys will have to put the finishing touches on your masterpieces before time runs out."

"If I try to embellish my picture any *more*," Marco groaned, trying to flesh out his smiley figure with a few more curves and shadows. "I'm going to cum on my paper. All this stimulation with the creamy food dye on the tip of my cock feels pretty good."

"Not as good as it's going to feel if one of us has a chance to *lick it off*," Emma grinned.

7

———

"Alright," Madison announced. "Brushes down, time's up. It's time to inspect your compositions and choose a winner."

The men stepped away from their paintings and turned around, revealing their bobbing erections coated with creamy paint.

"Are we talking about their drawings or their pretty *penises*?" Elle smiled.

"I think we should focus on their creations," Maddy said. "After all, the whole point of this exercise was to demonstrate that it's not so much about the *size* of the instrument as how they use it."

"Yes," Piper nodded. "If these paintings reflect their mastery in certain other areas, then I'd have to say some of these men are already masters of their craft."

"So it would seem," Madison said. "But there can only be one winner. Let's show our appreciation for their work by clapping while we appraise each piece. We'll begin with Marco's drawing."

The women clapped softly, wrinkling their foreheads at his messy stick figure.

"At least he tried to put some *meat* on the bones before he finished," Emma chuckled.

"What about Neil's piece?" Madison said, swinging her arm around to the next easel.

"His *heart* was in the right place," Trinity joked while the rest of us giggled at her double entendre.

"How about Ryan?" Madison said, turning toward his drawing of the naked mudflap girl.

"It's actually not a bad reproduction of the familiar icon," Lily said, tilting her head to the side. "But I don't know about you guys, I always *flinch* when I see that picture on the back of a trucker's rig."

"I agree," I said, peering at his picture with a scrunched face.

"Some of you seemed to appreciate *Diego's* drawing," Madison said, continuing to sweep her hand clockwise around the room.

"It's beautiful," Bonnie said as the rest of us clapped in approval. "Echoing Georgia O'Keeffe, it's beautiful and sensuous at the same time."

"And special marks for his flattering commentary," Elle nodded, smiling at Diego.

"What did you think of your *husband's* composition?" Madison said, pointing toward Toby's easel.

"It's pretty impressive, given the limited time he had to work with," Elle smiled. "I had no idea he was so versatile with his penis."

"I'm sure he'd jump at the chance to paint you with some *other* creamy substance if you'll let him," Laura grinned.

"Something tells me he's going to have plenty of chances before the night is over," Elle chuckled.

The women applauded loudly, smiling at Toby while they stared at his bobbing penis.

"What about *Shae*?" Madison said, pointing toward her pictogram.

"I like what her symbol represents," Trinity nodded while the rest of the women clapped softly. "It just doesn't have the same level of *detail* as some of the others."

"That only leaves *Lincoln* then," Madison said, turning toward Linc's easel.

Everybody paused while they took turns staring at his etching and his enormous erection.

"It demonstrates remarkable penmanship," Emma nodded.

"Or *pricks*manship," I chuckled, staring at his angled hard-on, dripping purple paint down the side of his long shaft.

"And the *message* is beautiful, also," Elle said while the rest of us clapped loudly.

"Alright, then," Madison said, turning back toward the men. "It seems to be a pretty close contest between Lincoln, Diego, and Toby. But based on the enthusiasm of your applause, I'd have to give the nod to *Toby*."

Each of the women stood up and cheered, clapping loudly while they peered at his Monet-inspired landscape.

"So, how do we decide which of us gets to clean him up?" Piper said, licking her lips.

"I suppose we could draw lots," Madison said, reaching into her game bag. "But I just happen to have this game wheel left over from one of my other parties. Why don't I spin the needle and see who it points to?"

Madison placed the spinner in the center of the coffee table in front of the sofa, then everyone leaned forward while she flicked the needle with the tip of her finger. After spinning around a few times, it finally stopped, pointing in the direction of one of the easels. The women followed the line of the arrow, tilting their heads slowly in the direction of Brad.

"It's pointing towards *Brad!*" Bonnie said. "I thought you said one of the *women* would have a chance to partner with the winner?"

"I didn't say that exactly," Madison grinned. "I only said it would be a randomly selected participant."

"But I've never been with a man that way before," Toby said, glancing uneasily at Brad.

"Neither had Brad before our last party," Maddy smiled. "But he seemed to warm up to the idea pretty quickly after the completion of the *Joystick Jenga* contest."

"It looks like you'll be kneeling in a slightly *different* position this time," Laura grinned at her husband. "You should be getting pretty used to it by now."

"What exactly do you expect him to *do* with me?" Toby said, peering at Madison with a wrinkled brow.

"Well, technically," Maddy said. "You only need to let him lick the dye off your penis. But depending on how much each of you *enjoy* the experience, there's no reason to stop there."

Elle suddenly cleared her throat, glancing up at her husband with a Cheshire Cat grin.

"We *did* say that we were coming to this party to spread our wings," she smiled. "I've had my chance, now it looks like it's going to be yours."

Toby sighed as he crossed his legs defensively.

"I didn't think when I drew two butterflies," he frowned. "That it might be two *male* butterflies."

8

———————

"**S**o where do you want me to do this?" Toby said, crossing his arms over his chest.

I found it interesting that as much as he pretended to dread the idea of receiving a gay blowjob, that his green-cream-coated dick was still standing straight up and bobbing excitedly overtop of his splattered stomach.

Looks like his little head is winning the battle with his big head, I chuckled to myself.

"Well, you've been standing up for the past ten minutes," Madison nodded. "Why don't you take a rest on the sofa, where Brad can get comfortable with you?"

"Okay..." Toby grumbled, walking slowing over to the couch as his hard-on swung from side to side.

When he sat on the cushion next to the side armrest, the rest of the group retreated toward the fireplace while Brad sat tentatively next to him, a few inches apart.

"How would you like me to do this?" he said, peering at Toby anxiously.

"I have no idea," Toby said, sitting with his knees

clamped tightly together and his erection jutting up between his legs. "I've never done anything like this before."

"Not with a *man*, perhaps," his wife grinned, slipping her fingers between her thighs while she stared at Toby's dripping hard-on from the edge of the fireplace hearth. "Why don't you close your eyes and imagine it's me licking your cock instead of Brad? You might even *enjoy* the experience if you open your mind a little bit."

"Yes," Bonnie nodded. "Like Shae suggested with her drawing, we *all* have some degree of attraction to the same sex. Didn't you experiment with some of your friends when you were younger?"

Toby took a deep sigh, refusing to answer the question, then he closed his eyes and tilted his head on the back of the sofa, spreading his legs slowly apart. Brad peered at his bobbing prick and paused while his own yellow-coated erection slapped up against his stomach.

"What are you waiting for, dear?" Laura teased. "You already had a little practice giving head to *Diego* at Madison's last party. This one should be even *tastier* with the creamy food dye coating Brad's cock."

Brad tilted his body slowly to the side and lowered his head toward Toby's erection, beginning to lick the side of his shaft with the end of his tongue. When his tongue reached the tip of his organ, Toby took a deep breath in, gripping the armrest tightly with his left hand.

"That's it, baby," Laura smiled, taking a seat next to Elle on the fireplace hearth so they could watch their husbands together. "I think Toby kind of *likes* it."

Brad darted his eyes at the two women rubbing their legs together on the fireplace, then he pressed his head forward a few more inches, angling his face to lick the other side of Toby's dick.

"Mmm," Laura groaned, staring at Toby's flaring erection. "That's fucking *hot*. Are you savoring this as much as I am, Elle?"

"I didn't think I'd enjoy watching two men having sex this much," Elle nodded, placing her left palm on top of Laura's knee while she watched the action. "Although I'm not sure Brad's going to be able to clean all the paint off Toby's dick from that position."

"I think she's right, honey," Laura said, slipping her hand inside Elle's parted thighs. "Why don't you *kneel* between Toby's legs so you're in a better position to lick it off?"

"Hmm," Brad nodded, growing increasingly excited watching the two women touching each other.

While Toby squinted with one eye half-open toward him, he slid off the sofa and positioned himself in front of his parted legs.

"*Yes*, baby," Laura hummed, sliding her hand further between Elle's thighs. "Lick his hard-on like it's a *popsicle*. A nice, juicy lemon-lime-flavored one."

Brad flattened his tongue and swiped it up the underside of Toby's pole, and Toby groaned, opening his eye a little further.

"Do you *like* that, sweetheart?" Elle grinned, pulling her left hand closer to Laura's dripping crotch. "Nobody said you couldn't *watch*. Why don't you open your eyes all the way and enjoy the show? Everybody *else* seems to be."

Toby raised his lids, glancing at the gallery of naked party guests touching themselves while they watched the two men on the sofa. When he saw Laura's and Elle's hands buried between each other's thighs, his eyes flared when Brad slid his tongue over his glans.

"*Mhhh,*" he moaned, lowering his eyes to watch Brad sucking the head of his dick.

"*Fuck*, yes," Elle grunted, rocking her hips in concert with her husband while the two women slowly fingered each other. "Suck him hard, Brad. That's fucking insane."

"Don't forget his *balls*, honey," Laura nodded, spreading her knees further apart while Elle slipped two fingers into her hole. "The paint is dripping down his shaft. I know how much you like it when I lick you there."

"Mmm," Brad nodded, lowering his head and sliding his tongue around Toby's tightening balls with mounting enthusiasm.

While he leaned over, licking Toby's cock and balls, I noticed his erection swinging between his legs, dripping yellow strings from his glans.

"Is that *paint* you're dripping onto the floor, Brad, or *pre-cum?*" Laura grinned, rocking her hips against Elle's probing fingers while she watched the erotic show on the sofa. "Because you seem to be enjoying this operation almost as much as Toby is."

"Mm-hmm," Brad nodded, placing his hand around his dick while he raised his head to suck on Toby's helmet again.

By now, Toby had both of his eyes wide open, alternating his gaze between the sight of the two married women fingering each other's dripping pussies and Brad's bobbing head over his hard-on. But this time, he moved his hands overtop of Brad's head, encouraging him to keep his focus on his sensitive glans while he groaned with increasing volume along with the women.

"Oh my God," Elle panted, raising her free hand to Laura's right breast and squeezing it hard. "This is the hottest thing I've ever seen. I'm going to come soon, watching this. Are you getting close, baby?"

"I am *now*," Toby grunted, pushing Brad's head further down over his cock.

"Take him *all the way*, like you did with Diego's cock," Laura groaned, circling her hand rapidly over Elle's darkening vulva while Elle finger-fucked her pussy. I think everybody is ready to come now. Show Toby what it's like to get a *real* gay blowjob."

Brad hesitated for a moment, then he relaxed his throat muscles while he lowered his head all the way down Toby's shaft, until his lips encircled the base of his pole just above his balls. While Toby throat-fucked him with white knuckles, Brad began to jerk his own dick faster while everybody in the room moaned in increasing excitement. When Toby suddenly lurched forward and began convulsing over Brad's bobbing head, Elle and Laura moaned out loud, pressing their fingers hard against each other's cunts while they jetted their juices over our thighs. Before long, everybody in the room was gasping and grunting as they climaxed along with the others.

When I saw Brad squirting thick strings of cum against the side of the sofa while he held his mouth over Toby's pulsing organ, I had to smile at Madison's suggestion this might actually clean things up. Between the splattering food dye from the men jerking their dicks while they watched Toby and Brad, and the women's dripping juices running down the insides of their legs, we'd only succeeded in making even *more* of a mess.

But what a beautiful mess it was, I smiled, watching the juices dripping out of Laura's and Elle's pussies while they squeezed each other's hands tightly between their legs.

9

———

"Well," Madison smiled after Brad lifted his head off Toby's dripping organ. "It looks like you managed to lick all the paint off his cock, but it seems that we've got a *different* kind of mess to clean up after now."

She reached into her game kit and pulled out a stack of hand towels, asking everyone to pass them around.

"If you could be so kind to clean up your mess, I'm going to go into the kitchen to prepare some more refreshments, then why don't we take a short break while we prepare for the next round?"

After a few minutes, the party guests began trickling into the kitchen, where we gathered around the island, nibbling on hors d'oeuvres.

"So," Elle said when she noticed her husband entering the room with a sheepish grin on his face. "Was it as awful as you imagined?"

Toby nodded with a lopsided smile, trying to avoid direct eye contact with Brad.

"Judging by how long he kept his dick planted on my

husband's face when he came," Laura chuckled. "I'd say he enjoyed it just fine."

"Was it as good as the blowjobs you usually get from *me*?" Elle said, raising an eyebrow.

Toby cocked his head to one side and simply smiled, signaling his satisfaction with the experience.

"It looks like I've still got a few things to learn," Elle grinned, nodding toward Brad. "Maybe same-sex partners really *do* know how to please one another better than mixed couples."

"*You* two certainly seemed to enjoy yourselves enough taking in the show," Toby said, nodding toward Laura and Elle. "Maybe you'll have a few more chances to hook up before the night is over."

"Speaking of," Bonnie said, peering toward Madison. "Isn't it the *women's* turn for some fun in the next contest?"

"Right you are, Bonnie," Maddy nodded. "In our next game I'm calling *Bobbing for Peaches*, each of the men will be competing to see who can get their partners off the fastest."

I couldn't help laughing at some of the names Madison had given the contests.

"I'm guessing based on the name of this one that they'll be doing this only with their mouths?" I chuckled.

"Yes," Maddy said. "Although, for the *winner* of the game, there'll be no limit on how your partner chooses to stimulate your peachka."

"How will we choose our partners *this* time?" Toby grunted. "Another spinning game wheel?"

"I thought to make it a little more interesting," Maddy smiled. "That I'd *blindfold* each of you."

"Both the men and the women?" Lily said.

"Mm-hmm," Madison nodded. "That way, nobody will know who's stimulating whom until it's over."

"Hmm," Laura grinned, peering around the table at each of the men as their penises began to take on a whole new life. "I like the sound of that."

"Once again," Shae huffed. "I seem to be the odd man out. With eight women and seven men, I suppose you want me to be on the *giving* end this time?"

"Not to worry," Madison said. "If you do a good enough job satisfying your partner, you'll have plenty of opportunities to get more involved in the second half of the game. Since you're the proud owner of *two* sets of sexual organs, you'll have more options than most as to how you choose to finish the exercise."

"Mmm," Shae nodded, her rising cock tapping against the underside of the kitchen island. "This contest is sounding more interesting by the moment."

"How will we know who comes first?" Marco said. "What if some of the women fake it?"

"Oh, I'll *know*," Madison grinned. "There are certain telltale signs that are impossible to hide. But to some degree, each of you will be on your honor. Besides, you'd just be doing your partner a disservice if you fake your orgasm. Otherwise, how will men ever learn how to eat pussy the proper way?"

"So we're only allowed to use our *mouths* to stimulate them?" Lincoln said.

"Yes," Madison nodded. "You'd have a bit of an unfair advantage if we allowed you to unleash that weapon of yours again."

"What about our *fingers?*" Brad said.

"Part of the purpose of this exercise is to learn how to use your mouths more creatively," Maddy said. "It's not just about flicking and sucking. It's about teasing and building up the excitement so your partner can enjoy the experience to the fullest."

Laura suddenly chuckled as she peered toward her husband.

"Are you sure you're going to be able to *find* the important parts with your eyes covered, sweetheart?" she said.

"I've never heard you complain before," Brad grinned.

"Can we talk to our partners while they stimulate us?" Piper asked. "If we want to teach them to be better lovers, doesn't it ultimately come down to better communication?"

"Maybe," Madison said. "But there's also something to be said for being more attuned to your partner's *body language*. Oftentimes, the experience is heightened by shutting out some of the other senses."

"Is that why we're wearing blindfolds?" Toby said.

"Partly," Madison nodded. "Besides helping with the random assignments, I think you'll find it to be a more interesting experience on both sides. Are you ready to get started?"

"Judging by how fast the boys have managed to get their *dicks* up again," Emma chuckled, glancing at the men's bobbing erections. "I'd have to take that as a yes."

10

———

When everybody returned to the living room, Madison instructed the women to sit side-by-side around the large sectional sofa then she gave everyone an individual blindfold, asking them to tie it tightly around their eyes so they couldn't see anything. Then she guided each of the men toward a random partner, pressing gently down on their shoulders until they kneeled on the floor. When I felt someone brush against my parted legs, I felt a dribble of lubrication spilling out of my pussy and trickling down the crack of my ass.

"Okay," Madison said, standing a few feet behind us. "In a few moments, we'll get started. But remember, although the prize goes to the one who climaxes first, that doesn't mean you should try to rush it. Just like in the story of the turtle and the hare, sometimes it's the *slow and steady* one who wins the race."

The room suddenly filled with silence while the redolent aroma of eight dripping pussies wafted under our noses.

"Alright, lady and gentlemen," Maddy announced. "Start your engines."

When I felt my partner's head lower between my legs, it didn't take long for me to recognize the familiar feel of Shae's curvy body pressing up against me. While she slid the tip of her tongue gently up the inside of my parted legs, I felt the ends of her long hair tickling my ankles and the sides of her soft breasts caressing the insides of my thighs.

"Mmm," I moaned, happy that Madison had matched the two of us again.

While she nibbled on the edges of my labia, I flashed back for a moment to the first time we'd bumped into one another at the local supermarket. Recognizing her from a cabaret show I'd attended earlier in the week, we joked about the size of the cucumbers we'd selected from the produce aisle, wondering what we intended to do with them. When I invited her out for coffee, the chemistry between us was undeniable, and it didn't take long for the two of us to head back to my house, where we made love for the rest of the afternoon. When I felt her naked under the covers for the first time, I was shocked and delighted when I discovered she had both male and female fully functioning sex organs. She was skilled and adept at using *all* of her tools, and I lost track of how many times she made me come that day.

But there was something about feeling her stimulating me while we were both *blindfolded* that heightened my excitement even more. While I listened to the sound of her mouth kissing and sucking my dripping pussy, I imagined her big hard-on bobbing between her legs, dripping pre-cum over the crown of her glans while her pussy dribbled juices down the inside of her thighs.

"Unghh," I groaned, as she flattened her tongue and

slowly swiped it all the way from my twitching anus to the tip of my folds.

Pausing overtop of my throbbing gland, she nodded her head up and down like she was licking an ice cream cone, blowing softly onto my burning bulb while I panted like a dog in heat a few inches above her body. By the time she encircled my jewel and began sucking on it with her puffy lips, I was already three-quarters of the way to the hardest orgasm I'd experienced in a long time.

As I listened to the sound of the others moaning and panting around me, it hardly mattered to me who came first. I just wanted to close my eyes and savor the feeling of this beautiful transgender woman giving me the sweetest pussy licking of my life. I smiled, imagining Madison standing behind all of us watching the sight of the men's asses raised in the air while each of us squirmed on the sofa, our hardening nipples and spreading sex flushes betraying our rising excitement. I envied her for a moment, but when Shae began drawing figure-eight patterns over my throbbing clit with the tip of her tongue, I grasped the back of her head tightly with two hands, pulling her face harder against my cunt.

Madison had said the *men* couldn't use their hands, but that didn't stop me from giving her some non-verbal feedback to keep doing what she was doing. While I felt my pleasure rising inexorably like an oncoming freight train, I slowly widened my legs, gaping my mouth open as I neared the tipping point. Shutting out the sounds of everything else in the room, when I felt my orgasm wash over me like a burst dam, I gushed my juices hard over her face buried between my legs, pressing her nose so hard against my spasming vulva that she could barely breathe. My orgasm seemed to last forever, and as I slowly began to become aware of the sounds of other women climaxing soon after, Shae hummed happily into my pussy while she cradled my ass gently in her hands.

Madison hesitated until the last of the women climaxed, then she glanced at her smartphone, nodding approvingly.

"That was quite a sight to behold," she said as the women panted in unison on the sofa and the men slowly raised their heads from their pussies, their erections bouncing excitedly between their legs. "Maybe you should practice this technique more frequently with your lovers. Because from *my* point of view, I've rarely seen a group of women more satisfied from the oral ministrations of their partners."

"Who was the winner?" Trinity said.

"Jade," Madison nodded, glancing at her timer. "And it took just over five minutes to get there. I was happy to see each of you taking your time and enjoying the *process* instead of just focusing on the destination."

"How can you be so sure she was the one who came *first?*" Laura said. "Because from where I was sitting, there was a whole lot of moaning going on all around me."

"Jade has a unique way of demonstrating when she climaxes, aren't I right, Shae?" Madison said.

"Mmm," Shae smiled, licking my juices off the sides of her mouth while her breasts glistened from the spray I'd jetted on her chest. "She squirts even harder than *I* do when I come."

Elle suddenly shifted restlessly on the sofa, tugging on her bandana.

"Does that mean we can take our blindfolds off now?" she said. "Because I'd like to watch them finish up, not to mention find out who was sucking my pussy so expertly."

"Absolutely," Madison nodded, eager to move on to the next phase of the contest.

When each of the participants flipped off their bandanas, they smiled at their partners, nodding in excitement with who they'd been paired up with. Once again, Madison had expertly mixed up the matches so everyone had a chance to hookup with a new partner, and I had to laugh at how well she'd organized the whole event.

"Something tells me these pairings you've been setting us up with aren't nearly as *random* as you're leading us to believe," I chuckled.

"Just trying to spread the love around," Madison grinned, revealing a dark stain in the crotch of her jeans as she shifted position.

"It looks like we weren't the *only* ones enjoying that last exercise," I said. "It seems a little unfair that you get to soak it all up while the rest of us are kept in the dark."

"I didn't hear you complaining while you were coming all over Shae's face," Madison grinned, stepping out of her wet clothes. "But now that you mention it, I'm looking forward to enjoying the rest of the show almost as much as the rest of you."

11

"How do you want us to *finish* the exercise?" Shae said, leaning back as a large drop of pre-cum slid down the underside of her bobbing prick.

"It looks like you're about ready to explode along with the rest of the men," Maddy smiled, glancing down at her flaring cock. "It's only fair that *both* of you should have an opportunity to enjoy the experience equally this time,"

"I almost came when I felt Jade squirting all over my face," Shae nodded. "I'd love to dip my tool in her well if she's willing."

"Are you kidding me?" I grunted, leaning forward to lick my juices off her hardening nipples. "I've been dreaming of riding that cock ever since I watched you drawing that picture on the easel."

Brad cleared his throat, peering at his partner Piper's tumescent pussy lips while she dribbled juices out of her slit.

"Are we allowed to hookup with *our* partners too?" he said.

"As much as I'm sure all of you would like to," Madison

said. "In the interests of keeping the contest fair, I think we should continue to play by the rules. There can only be one winner this time."

"That doesn't stop us from touching *ourselves* while we watch them make love, does it?" Neil said, caressing the tip of his pole.

"I suppose not," Madison smiled. "But you might want to save some for the next game coming up after this. Because in the contest called *Firing Range*, the more primed your pump will be, the better chance you'll have of capturing your prize once it's over."

"Fair enough," Neil nodded, pulling his hand away from his cock. "Because I'm pretty pumped after licking Emma's pussy."

"Save that thought and you'll have your chance to blow your wad soon enough. But for now, why don't each of us relax while we watch Jade and Shae consummate their connection in a more intimate way."

"Mmm," Shae said, smiling toward me. "Is there any particular way you'd like to have me?"

"I'd like to have you *every* way," I grinned, running my eyes over her glistening breasts, toward her flexing hard-on and dripping pussy. "But right now, I just want you *inside* me. If you don't put that pretty prick inside my pussy soon, I liable to come all over you again just *looking* at you."

"You don't have to ask twice," Shae said, pressing her hips forward, pointing her flexing phallus toward my opening.

I reached out to grasp the tip of it, swiping it up and down my dripping vulva, and she groaned when she felt my soft lips caressing the sensitive glans of her penis.

"Talk about coming just *watching* you," she grunted. "If

you keep teasing me like that, I'm going to make almost as much of a mess as you just did."

"Well, we can't have that," I grinned, pushing my hips forward as her crown slipped inside my slit. "I want to feel you coming *inside* me."

"Fuck, yes," Shae hissed, burying her cock slowly inside me. "I don't know which I enjoy more, feeling you squirt all over my *face* or my *cock* when you come."

"I'm pretty sure I can *guess* which you prefer," I chuckled, leaning forward to rub my tits against hers while I drifted my hand around the back of her ass. "I want to feel your pussy throbbing when you come inside me."

"Oh *God*," Shae hissed when she felt my fingers sliding inside her hole. "That feels so good. Play with my pussy while I fuck you."

"Holy shit," Toby suddenly groaned, while he stared at the two of us making out.

"You like that, baby?" his wife grinned, glancing toward his cock straining up against his stomach. "Maybe you'd like to play with a *different* kind of cock next time?"

"Or her *pussy*," Toby nodded, dry-humping the air in front of his partner Trinity.

"Having twice the equipment makes it twice the fun," I smiled, squeezing Shae's tits while she fucked me with her big dick.

"Mhhh," she groaned, pressing her face forward to kiss me. "Keep fingering me like that. I can feel it coming. I'm going to come so hard inside you."

"Yes, baby," I panted, feeling my own pleasure rapidly rising. "I'm going to come with you. Ride me like a horse."

While Shae dug the tips of her fingers harder into the sides of my ass as she pounded her instrument deep inside me, I began to feel the inside of her pussy tenting open, preparing to spasm in orgasmic contractions. Although she had a fully functioning penis, I found it fascinating how she seemed like a woman in every other respect, from her pretty face to her natural breasts to her pulsating pussy. But there was something about having her hard *tool* inside me that took her lovemaking to an entirely new level. I'd enjoyed plenty of strap-on dildos with my lesbian lovers over the years, but feeling a real-life, throbbing, burning erection inside me while I squeezed her pretty tits was something nobody else could duplicate.

Suddenly, she arched her back and threw her head back, gaping her mouth open as a deep flush rolled over her cheeks, squealing in ecstasy while she emptied her seed deep inside my pussy. When we both began squirting our juices between our parted legs, everybody in the room groaned, hardly believing what they were watching. But while the two of us held each other tightly, convulsing in the throes of a powerful mutual climax, I noticed Madison standing a short distance behind us, peering at our two pussies while she thrust three fingers deep into her snatch.

It looks like more than two can play this game, I smiled, happy to see her joining the fun along with the rest of the group.

12

"Mmm," Madison said, pulling her fingers out of her dripping pussy. "These games are getting more exciting by the moment."

"I thought you said we couldn't *play* with ourselves?" Neil huffed.

"I only said the *men* couldn't," Maddy smiled.

"It hardly seems fair," Marco protested. "I'm about to *explode* from watching that hot hookup."

"That's exactly the way I wanted it," Maddy nodded. "Because in our next contest named *Firing Range*, you're going to have a chance to put all your pent-up energy to good use."

"Are we going to be aiming at another target like in the bullseye contest from your last party?" Linc said.

"You won't be focusing on a specific *target* per se," Madison grinned, peering down at Lincoln's bobbing organ, already rock-hard from watching Shae and me. "In this game, *distance* will be more important than aim. So you've already got a few inches head start on the rest of the field."

"What did you have in mind, exactly?" Diego said, wrinkling his forehead.

Madison reached into her bag and pulled out a thick roll of pink parchment paper, laying it in long strips in front of the fireplace. Then she dragged the sofa back a few feet and asked the men to stand in front of it, side-by-side.

"You guys said you wanted to *touch* yourselves in the last round," she smiled. "Well, here's your big chance. In this contest, we're going to see how far you can shoot your wad. The man who fires the furthest wins the prize."

"What's the prize?" Toby said.

"This time, I'm going to let you *choose* who you'd like to hook-up with. That is, assuming the women are willing."

"Oh, I'm willing, alright," Laura grinned. "I haven't had so much fun playing musical chairs since Kindergarten."

"Who says it has to be a *woman*?" Ryan said, placing his hands on his hips.

"Good point, Ryan," Madison nodded. "We *did* say to park your mental blocks at the door. We've already seen enough boy-on-boy and girl-on-girl pairings to spark everyone's imagination."

Shae suddenly cleared her throat, crossing her arms defiantly.

"Which side of the contest do you want *me* to be on this time?" she said. "I'm not really either a boy or a girl."

"You've got a *cock*, don't you?" Maddy grinned. "Let's see if you've got the right stuff."

"I'm not sure how much more I've got left to deliver after coming so hard with Jade," Shae smiled. "But I'll give it my best shot."

"Speaking of," Brad said. "How will we know who shot the furthest?"

Madison reached into her game kit and pulled out a

small pad of Post-it notes, scribbling each contestant's name on the slips and handing one to each of the women.

"Each of you will have a counterpart who'll be responsible for recording the landing points of your cumshots by placing a marker with your name beside the target. I've chosen pink-colored paper to help identify the spots, since the color should change to dark red with the extra moisture. But you better be careful ladies, you might have to sidestep the volleys of spunk if everybody comes at the same time."

"Holy shit," Lily said, shaking her head. "This is insane! Where do you come up with these ideas?"

"I've seen enough guys jerk off in my day," Madison smiled. "I thought it might be kind of fun to compare their technique while we give them a chance to relieve their purple balls."

"Hmm," Laura nodded. "While we come up with a few new ideas for giving them better handies."

"Exactly," Madison said. "If nothing else, I hope this party has expanded your repertoire of skills you can use with your partners."

"To say the *least*," Elle grinned, glancing at her husband standing beside the other men while their flagpoles stood waving in front of their bellies. "I had no idea it would open so many doors for Toby and me when we agreed to come."

"Speaking of *coming*," Madison said, turning toward the lineup of grinning men. "Are you guys ready to get started?"

"I'm not sure I've seen eight men more eager to get started in my whole life," Laura chuckled.

WHILE MADISON TOOK up position beside the men to signal for them to begin, I glanced at the row of bobbing erections with a giant smile. Each of them was a different size, color, and shape, and it echoed back to the first contest of the evening, when the men used the Rorschach blots to match each of the women's pussies to their owner.

Marco's and Neil's cocks were uncircumcised, with their pink crowns partially exposed like two piggies in a blanket. Diego and Marco had a warm caramel color to their instruments, making them look like bronze sculptures. Lincoln's huge, slightly curved black organ looked like an enormous sausage, ready for the licking. Only *Shae's* prick looked somewhat out of place, with her dripping pussy sitting under her flaring erection instead of two balls.

But *everyone's* erection looked proud and capable standing at full mast, twitching in the still air while each of the women looked on with fascination.

"Alright," Madison smiled, glancing at their bobbing dicks and lowering her arm. "This contest isn't timed, so feel free to take your time and enjoy the experience to the fullest. As with the turtle and the hare, you might well find that the slower the build-up, the greater the reward."

Each of the men grabbed their hard-ons and began stroking them softly, darting their eyes between the cocks of the other men and the line-up of women who'd assembled at the side of the runway to mark their results. I found it mesmerizing to watch each of their techniques, somewhat surprised by how different they varied from one man to another. Some of the men only stroked the sensitive end of their penis, while others gripped the entire shaft of their organs with a balled fist, jerking their poles hard while they rocked their hips forward and back. And some of them caressed their balls with one hand while they stroked their penis with their other, while some of the better *endowed* men held their cock with two hands as they flexed their buttocks, poking their dripping heads out the end while they stared at their manhood, moaning softly.

It didn't take long for each of the *women* to get into the mood along with the men, and before long, we were rolling our fingers absent-mindedly over our clits while we watched the men fapping their dicks.

"Don't get too distracted by the entertainment, ladies," Madison kidded. "Remember, you're going to have to act quickly when your partner pops off."

"We can do two things at once," I grinned, glancing at the other women standing on opposite sides of the parchment paper. "It's kind of like watching porn on a slow day at work. We've got to find *something* to do while we wait for the big finish."

"It shouldn't be much longer now," Neil huffed, jerking his darkening tool faster while his balls slowly tightened around the base of his shaft.

"Mmm, yes, baby," Bonnie purred, holding his tag softly in her hand. "Let it rip and show us what you've got."

"Nnghh," he suddenly groaned, pressing his hips forward while he squeezed his shaft, jetting a string of jizz in a long arc toward the fireplace.

When his first volley landed halfway down the landing strip, Bonnie paused until each of his successive spurts plopped in progressively shorter distances down the runway. When he finally finished spurting, she stepped gingerly onto the pad, placing her note beside the first shot, then she quickly stepped back to the relative safety of the viewing gallery.

"I might be the lucky one having my partner shoot first," she smiled, nodding to the paper, stained with seven dark blotches. "Things could get pretty *slippery* over there in another couple of minutes."

"Oh God," Marco suddenly growled, gripping his dick tightly between two hands, his glans now fully exposed from his retracted foreskin. "I'm going to come—oh *fuckkk...*"

This time, his spunk jetted out in a straight line while he held his throbbing dick level with the floor, his semen sliding along the paper as it landed, leaving a trail like a slug.

But his marker Emma made the mistake of stepping onto the mat too quickly, and as she bent over to mark his first landing spot, his second shot caught her square on the side of her cheek.

"Ew!" she squealed, quickly recoiling and wiping her face with the side of her arm while she retreated back to the side of the runway.

"You better wait until they finish dropping their load next time," Laura chuckled, winking toward Emma. "It looks like their first shot isn't always their *best* shot."

"I'll have to remember that," Emma grinned, wiping her slippery arm against the side of her ass.

One by one, each of the men grunted and groaned in succession, tightening their faces and tensing their bodies while they spurted their spunk in a volley of streams along the runway.

"This is better than watching the Bellagio fountain in Las Vegas," Laura chuckled, sprinting between the salvos to mark her partner's shot.

"And the canvas is almost as interesting as a *Pollock* painting," Trinity said, nodding toward the pattern of random speckled dots on the paper.

"This is absolutely brilliant," Bonnie agreed, watching the men's cocks spasming as they spurted long ropes of jizz all over the parchment. "Who would have thought it would be so much fun watching a group of men jacking off together?"

"Yeah," Piper said. "Screw the *circle jerk*, it's way more interesting watching them trying to outdo one another."

"That only leaves Toby and Lincoln left to pop off," I said, glancing toward the two remaining men still stroking their hard-ons.

The women's gaze turned back toward the sofa, where Toby and Linc were holding their breath as a deep flush began to roll over their flexing pecs. It was interesting to see Lincoln pounding his big dick between his hands almost like he was fucking an inanimate object, while Toby rolled his right hand softly over his purple crown while he squeezed his balls with his other hand. Before long, Lincoln began grunting like a wild boar, squirting his first shot all the way to the base of the fireplace hearth. I waited until he finished coming, then I quickly placed my marker beside his wet spot near the fireplace, rejoining the rest of the women as we watched Toby's face becoming redder and redder.

"It looks like you're going to have an *aneurism*," his wife said, peering at him with wide eyes. "Just let it go, baby. You're starting to worry me."

His entire body tensed up, then his mouth slowly yawned open while he stared straight ahead in a catatonic trance. When his cream finally flew out of the tip of his cock, the first shot landed with a loud plop on the face of the fireplace just below the mantle. Most of his strings landed further than the other men's, even Lincoln's, until his spurts slowly began to subside, landing closer to his feet. By the time he finished, I counted twelve new spots on the canvas, nodding approvingly.

"Holy *fuck*, Elle," I said, turning toward his wife. "Your husband is a beast. Does he *always* shoot that hard?"

"Not that I've noticed before," Elle grinned. "Maybe the sight of eight women watching him jerk off gave him a little extra motivation."

"Or maybe he's already thinking about who he'd like to hook up with in the next round," Laura smiled.

13

W hile the men stood next to each other with their half-erect penises dripping strings of cum onto the floor, Madison turned toward the women and smiled.

"I don't think we need the markers to tell us who won," she grinned, glancing at the large stain on the front of the fireplace. "That was a pretty impressive performance, Toby. I don't think your swimmers even need *tails* to find their way to their target with a cannon like that to shoot from. I'm surprised you and Elle only have two children!"

"It's a good thing I'm on birth control," Emma nodded. "Although after that demonstration, I'm thinking maybe we should *double up* on our protection."

Madison laughed, then she turned toward Toby.

"Do you think you've got enough gas left in the tank to run a few more laps?" she said. "Who would you like to partner up with to claim your prize?"

"I think I need a few more moments to recover," Toby said, holding his hands on his knees while he bent over, panting heavily.

"Not based on how erect your cock is," Elle joked, peering between his legs at his flaring erection. "You must have somebody *special* in mind if you're still this hard after coming so strong."

"Maybe he's thinking about another gay blowjob," Trinity laughed.

"I'm thinking about someone with a *cock* alright," Toby grinned. "But not another man. I'd love to have a chance to hook up with Shae if she's still up for it."

"I *knew* it," Elle chuckled. "The way you've been staring at her all night, it's hardly a surprise."

"But it's not so bad if it's with another *woman* this time, is it?" he said with a lopsided smile.

"Perhaps you'd like to *join* the two of us?" Shae said, glancing toward Elle. "With all of my body parts, there's more than enough to go around."

"Really?" Elle said, raising her eyebrows at the thought of having a three-way with her husband and the sexy ladyboy. "How would we do that exactly? Won't we be tied up like a *pretzel*?"

"Well, we'd have to position ourselves carefully," Shae laughed. "But it's not like I haven't done this before. I'm equally adept at making love with both men and women."

"Jesus, babe," Toby said, bulging his eyes as he peered toward his wife. "That sounds fucking hot. Plus, it's not cheating if we do it *together*."

"I'm game if you are," Elle smiled, noticing Shae's organ slowly rising again between her legs. "But who's going to put what *where*? With so many cocks and holes to choose from, it seems like a bit of a crap shoot."

"Well, Toby's already experienced what it's like to be with another man," Shae said. "How about if he samples my lady part this time, while you go for a ride on my cock?"

"Okay," Elle said, furrowing her brow. "But I'm still having a hard time picturing it..."

"Tell you what," Shae smiled. "Let's make this simple. Why don't we have Toby lie down on the floor face-up while I sit on his cock, facing toward his chest. Then you can in turn sit on *my* cock, facing in whichever direction you prefer."

"Mmm," Elle hummed, picturing the scene as a dribble of lubrication trickled down the inside of her thigh. "That sounds hot. Which way would you like me to face, sweetheart–toward Shae or towards you?"

"Hmm," Toby nodded, pausing for a moment while he considered the options. "As much as like the idea of you two rubbing your tits together while Shae fucks you, I think I'd enjoy it even *more* watching the expression on your face while she fucks you from behind."

"Works for me," Elle said, sliding her fingers over her dripping pussy and raising them to her mouth to lick them teasingly. "But you better assume the position quickly, because I'm already dripping like a faucet imagining what this is going to feel like."

Toby glanced at Madison to make sure she was okay with the slight change of plans, and when she nodded silently, he brushed the sheets of parchment paper off to the side of the fireplace, then he lay down on the hardwood floor with his bouncing prick pointing toward his face.

"I'll have some of that," Shae nodded, taking this as her invitation.

She walked over in front of him and placed her feet on either side of his hips, then slowly lowered her pussy over his throbbing erection.

"Mmm," she groaned, taking Toby's dick all the way

inside her hole. "I don't often get enough attention to my girly parts. Everybody seems to only want a piece of my *cock*."

"Well, it's a very pretty one indeed," Toby said, tilting his head forward and grasping it gently with two hands. "To match the *rest* of your beautiful body."

"Ohh," Laura sighed, staring at the handsome couple joined at the hip. "That's so sweet. Are you guys sure you don't want *another* one in the mix?"

"Back off, bitch," Elle joked, pushing Laura aside playfully. "She's mine. My husband won her fair and square. Just sit back and enjoy the show."

"Mmm," Shae purred, watching Elle strut in front of the fireplace. "That is one *sweet* ass. No wonder Toby shoots as far as he does. I would *too* if I had that to come home to every night."

"Well, *tonight*," Elle grinned, stamping her feet on either side of Toby's torso while she dripped her juices onto his bare chest. "He's going to be coming home to something different. And I'm going to be there to *watch* him."

She bent slowly forward at the waist, angling her pussy toward Shae's face, and Shae leaned toward her, licking her tongue between her legs, swiping it softly all the way from the base of her mound to her tight pucker.

"Mmm," Elle groaned as she grinned at her husband. "Are you sure I can't sit on her *face* instead of her cock while you fuck her?"

"Whichever you prefer, babe," Toby smiled while squeezing her swinging tits. "I can bring it home either way."

"Well, we can't let *you* have all the fun, can we?" she smiled, lowering her hips until she felt the tip of Shae's hard-on pressing up against her lips.

Shae grabbed the side of her ass and guided it further down, slowly inserting her erection in Elle's pussy while Elle spread her knees over Brad's stomach.

"Oh, *fuckkk*," Elle groaned, flaring her eyes while she stared at her husband. "This is insane. We've got to come to these parties more often."

"That's fine by me," Madison moaned, circling her clit as she watched the three lovers making out on the floor.

"And *me*," Laura nodded.

"And me..." Piper agreed.

"I think it's *unanimous*," Madison laughed, glancing around the room at the group of men and women nodding enthusiastically while they rubbed their crotches in growing arousal.

"*Fuck* me, Shae," Elle suddenly grunted, placing the palms of her hands on Toby's flexing pecs while Shae rocked her hips from behind. "I want to watch the look on my husband's face while you pound me."

"And while he pounds *me*," Shae groaned, gripping Elle's ass tightly in her hands.

"Yes," Toby moaned, watching the two women rolling their bodies over his hips. "This is the hottest thing I've ever seen."

"Even from your porn stash?" Elle joked.

"It's a million times better in real life," Toby nodded. "I didn't even know it was *possible* for three people to hook up like this."

"That's because I'm one in a million," Shae panted, slipping her hands around the front of Elle's body and squeezing her breasts while she fucked her tight ass. "There's not many transgender girls that have both a cock and a pussy."

"Are you sure we can't take you *home* with us to play with you more often?" Elle grunted, curling her fingertips into Toby's skin while she felt her pleasure slowly beginning to rise. "Because I can imagine a whole *slew* of sexy combinations the three of us could get into if we had more time."

"Just give me the word and I'll be at your doorstep in a flash," Shae nodded, feeling her own orgasm beginning to build inside her.

"Mmm," Toby said, rising up off the floor and bending forward to kiss his wife while he and Shae rocked their hips together in unison. "I'm going to come again soon, baby. Do you think you can come with me?"

"*Fuck* yes," Elle panted, sliding her hands around his back and squeezing his flexing buttocks. "Empty your seed in Shae's sweet pussy. I'm just about there."

"That makes *three* of us," Shae grunted, gripping Elle's tits tightly in her hands as she passed over the tipping point.

"*Mmftt,*" she suddenly hissed, slapping the sides of her thighs against Elle's buttocks while she exhaled heavily on her back.

"Oh God, Toby," Elle rasped. "I can feel her cumming inside me. Let it go, baby. I'm ready to come. It feels so good..."

Toby stretched his arms around the back of Shae's shoulders and pulled the three of them tighter together, then he grunted into Elle's mouth while he kissed her passionately.

"*Nngah!*" he growled, feeling his cock pulsing hard inside Shae's dripping pussy while his wife convulsed over Shae's organ.

I was so busy watching the three of them have the hottest sex I'd seen in a long time, that I completely lost track of where I was. But as I listened to the sound of the other party guests climaxing while they played with their cocks and pussies, I smiled, happy to savor the sight of everyone else lost in a moment of rapture while I experienced my own version of quiet nirvana.

14

"That was crazy-hot," I grinned after everyone came down from their highs.

"It *was* kind of fun, wasn't it?" Madison said while streams of lubrication dribbled down the insides of her thighs.

"I can't imagine how you're going to top the last contest where all the guys shot off together."

"What if *everyone* has a chance to come this time?" Maddy smiled.

"I don't know how you could possibly arrange that," I said, pinching my eyebrows together.

"Well, half of the fun in the last contest was watching the men while they stimulated themselves. What if we could see *everybody's* faces while they hooked up? In this next contest named *Orgasm Face*, we're going to do just that."

"You mean everyone's going to have a chance to hook up with each other at the *same time*?" Piper said.

"It's starting to get a bit late," Madison nodded, peering at her watch. "I think the best way to end our party with a bang is to finish with a *different* kind of big bang."

Then she peered at some of the men still standing with their dicks in their hands.

"But to get started, I first need a couple of volunteers to help me move a few things around."

Ryan and Marco nodded their heads, then Madison escorted them up to the second floor, where she asked them to carry the large stand-up mirror in her bedroom downstairs. When they returned to the living room, she instructed them to lay it horizontally at the base of the fireplace, then she placed eight cushions on the floor a few feet in front of the mirror.

"I'm guessing it's the *women's* turn to get on their knees this time?" Trinity said, inspecting the unusual arrangement.

"Actually, *everybody* will be on their knees in this final game," Madison smiled. "While the women rest on their hands and knees facing the mirror, the men will crouch behind them, watching their faces while they fuck them doggy-style."

"And while we watch *their* faces," Emma nodded.

"Exactly," Madison said. "It's a little bit like the house of mirrors at the county fair, except in *this* case you'll have something a little more interesting to keep yourselves amused."

"How will we choose our partners this time?" Bonnie said.

"To keep with the theme of random pairings," Madison said, scribbling some notes on a Post-it pad and handing the slips out to each contestant. "I've marked each of your slips with either a number or a letter. Number one will match up with letter A, number two will match up with letter B, and so on."

Everybody glanced at their slips, then they peered curiously around the room, wondering who they were going to be paired up with.

"Are the women designated with *letters or numbers*?" Shae said.

"Letters," Madison nodded.

"So that means I'm joining the *men* again?" she frowned.

"Only because there's eight women and seven men," Maddy smiled. "Otherwise, you'd be the odd man out."

"Story of my life," Shae chuckled.

"What will *you* be doing while all this is going down?" Laura said. "It doesn't look like this game requires any *officiating* this time."

"I'm just going to stand back and enjoy the show," Maddy grinned. "I'll have a unique perspective none of the rest of you have. While you're watching each other's *faces* in the mirror, I'll be watching your pussies and asses while the men pound you from behind."

"I'm beginning to see why you planned these parties," Elle chuckled. "You get your pick of the premium viewing spots."

"And with an odd number of *men and women*," Shae nodded. "When she gets to slip into the *action*."

"What can I say?" Madison grinned. "I'm just a lonely girl looking for some new ways to spice up my love life."

"Well, feel free to join us any time," Shae said. "I'm sure we can find some way to accommodate one more in the mix to make sure *everyone* walks away with a happy ending."

"Maybe I will," Madison smiled, peering down at the cushions. "But for now, I want each of the women to kneel on the cushions from left to right, starting with letter A. Then the men will take up position behind them, matching the correct numbers with the letters."

After all of the women rested on the cushions, I was

excited to see Toby kneel behind me, eager to feel his pulsing tool inside me.

"Are you sure you're going to be able to get it *up* one more time?" his wife Elle kidded. "What will this be, the *third* time you've come tonight?"

"Four, actually," Toby smiled, peering at my dripping pussy. "But after seeing how Jade squirts when she comes, I'm *already* getting excited just thinking about it."

"Enjoy, baby," Elle grinned, glancing in the mirror while Brad kneeled behind her. "It looks like it'll be *my* turn to pair up with Brad this time. Let's hope he's as talented with his *dick* as he is with his mouth."

"Mmm," Laura hummed, widening her eyes when she saw Shae nestling up behind her with her dripping cock. "Looks like I'm finally going to have a chance to hook up with Shae. I have to hand it to Madison, she really knows how to encourage *mingling* at her parties."

Everybody chuckled while they smiled at their partners, then Madison gave the go-ahead to get started.

"Alright," she smiled. "What are you guys waiting for? Those pussies aren't going to fuck *themselves*."

The men peered down at their partners' asses, then they grabbed the tips of their cocks, pointing them toward the women's dripping holes. When they inserted them inside their pussies, each of the women moaned, watching their partners in the mirror as their faces began to flush. While their bodies began to rock back and forth, I darted my eyes along the length of the mirror, watching their tits shaking on their chests and the men's abs flexing while they pounded their pussies from behind. Everybody seemed just as interested in what everyone *else* was doing, and as their eyes flitted between the twisting bodies, it seemed like a voyeur's dream.

But when I noticed Madison standing alone, rubbing her pussy gently while she watched everyone grunting and moaning, I signaled for her to join Toby and me in front of the fireplace. When she strolled over next to us, I instructed her to sit on the raised hearth in front of my head, then I buried my face between her knees, eagerly lapping up her juices. Before long, everybody in the room was panting and groaning, edging closer to another collective orgasm.

Laura was the first one to climax as she stared at Shae's bouncing tits while she tilted her hips, pressing her pulsing organ deep inside her pussy. Then Brad came soon after, watching his wife groaning on the end of her dick, and before long, the entire room was filled with the glorious sound of seventeen friends climaxing together while they watched each other's faces twisting in delirious pleasure. Madison waited until everybody else climaxed, and when I felt her hips begin to convulse over my face, I too lost all control, jetting my juices all over Toby's tightening balls while he gripped my ass, shooting his wad hard inside me.

When everybody finally finished shaking and groaning, we all collapsed in a giant heap on top of the cushions, laughing and caressing each other's dripping bodies. Madison's carnival-themed party had been a giant hit, and I was already thinking ahead to what she would dream up next.

READY FOR MORE EROTIC chills and thrills? Read the next volume in Jade's Erotic Adventures, *Dreamscape. Buy direct and save at victoriarusherotica. Or download from your favorite online bookstore here: retailer links.*

Where all your wildest fantasies come to life...

ALSO BY VICTORIA RUSH

Adult Fairytales:

The Enchanted Forest: An Erotic Fairytale

The Land of Giants: An Erotic Fairytale

The Dragon's Lair: An Erotic Fairytale

Witch's Brew: An Erotic Fairytale

The Mage's Spell: An Erotic Fairytale

The Mermaid Lagoon: An Erotic Fairytale

The Coven: An Erotic Fairytale

Rapunzel: An Erotic Fairytale

The Seven Dwarfs: An Erotic Fairytale

The Land of Mutants: An Erotic Fairytale

The Erotic Temple: A Sexy Fairytale (Coming Soon)

Erotica Themed Bundles:

Voyeur: Lesbian Erotica Bundle

Public Affairs: A Lesbian Anthology

Futa Fantasies: The Ladyboy Collection

Threesomes: The Lesbian Collection

Threesomes - Volume 2: The Lesbian Collection

First Time: A Lesbian Anthology

Hedonism: An Erotic Anthology

Switch Hitters: Bisexual Erotica

Taboo Erotica: The Lesbian Series

BDSM: The Lesbian Collection

Party Games: The Erotic Collection

Party Games 2: The Erotic Collection

All Girl 1: Lesbian Erotica Bundle

All Girl 2: Lesbian Erotica Bundle

All Girl 3: Lesbian Erotica Bundle

All Girl 4: Lesbian Erotica Bundle

Erotic Fairytale Bundles:

Clover's Fantasy Adventures: Books 1 - 5

Clover's Fantasy Adventures: Books 6 - 10

Erotic Fantasy:

Pirate's Bounty: A Time Travel Adventure

Wild West: A Time Travel Adventure

Private Riley: A Time Travel Adventure

Cleopatra's Secret: A Time Travel Adventure

Bounty Hunter 2125: A Time Travel Adventure

Ninja Assassin: A Time Travel Adventure

The 300: A Time Travel Adventure

Arabian Nights: An Erotic Fairytale (coming soon...)

Steamy Time Travel Bundles:

Riley's Time Travel Adventures: Books 1 - 5

Lesbian Erotica:

The Dinner Party: Lesbian Voyeur Erotica

The Darkroom: Bisexual Voyeur Erotica

Naked Yoga: Lesbian Transgender Erotica

Nude Cruise: Bisexual Voyeur Erotica

Rush Hour: Taboo Public Sex

The Girl Next Door: First Time Lesbian Erotic Romance

Girls' Camp: Lesbian Group Sex

Wet Dream: Ladyboy Fantasy Erotica

The Convent: Taboo Sex with a Nun

Sex Robot: A Dream Sex Machine

The Personal Trainer: Getting Pumped at the Gym

The Dominatrix: BDSM Lesbian Domination

Webcam Chat: Lesbian Online Sex

Paint Me: A Kinky Bodypainting Workshop

The Toy Party: Girls Sharing Sex Toys

The Costume Party: Strapping One On

Swedish Sauna: Lesbian Group Sex

The Therapist: Taboo Lesbian Erotica

Elevator Shaft: Bisexual Threesomes Erotica

Ladyboy: Lesbian Transgender Erotica

Peep Show: Lesbian Voyeur Erotica

The Dare: Public Sex Erotica

Maid Service: Lesbian Threesomes Erotica

The Hitchhiker: First Time Lesbian Erotica

The Housesitter: Spycam Lesbian Erotica

The Spa: Lesbian Group Orgy

Parlor Games: Blindfold Sex Party

The Exchange Student: First Time Lesbian Erotica

The Hostel: Bisexual Group Erotica

The Harem: Lesbian Erotic Romance

The Orient Express: Lesbian Voyeur Erotica

The First Lady: A Forbidden Lesbian Erotic Romance

The Slave: Lesbian BDSM Erotica

The Masseuse: Lesbian Sensuous Erotica

Too Close for Comfort: Lesbian Forbidden Erotica

Naked Twister: A Wild Party Game

Lexi: The Sex App (Lesbian Fantasy Erotica)

Call Girl: Lesbian Bisexual Threesomes Erotica

Circle Jill: Lesbian Masturbation Workshop

The Viewing Room: Masturbation Voyeur Erotica

Spin the Bottle: A Kinky Party Game

The Hair Salon: Lesbian Voyeur Erotica

Tribadism 1: Girls Only Sex Workshop

Tribadism 2: The Art of Scissoring

Tribadism 3: Threeway Hookups

The Kiss: A Game of Oral Sex

Pledge Week: Sorority Sisters

Carny Games 1: A Wild Sex Party

Carny Games 2: A Kinky Sex Party

Carny Games 3: An Erotic Sex Party

Dreamscape: An Artificial Reality Game

Glory Hole: Guess Who's On the Other Side

Joy Ride: A Late Night Erotic Bus Trip

The Blind Girl: An Erotic Romance(Coming Soon)

Lesbian Erotica Bundles:

Jade's Erotic Adventures: Books 1 - 5

Jade's Erotic Adventures: Books 6 - 10

Jade's Erotic Adventures: Books 11 - 15

Jade's Erotic Adventures: Books 16 - 20

Jade's Erotic Adventures: Books 21 - 25

Jade's Erotic Adventures: Books 26 - 30

Standalone Stories:

The Polynesian Girl: A Lesbian EroticRomance

FOLLOW VICTORIA RUSH:

Want to keep informed of my latest erotic book releases? Sign up for my newsletter and receive a FREE bonus book:

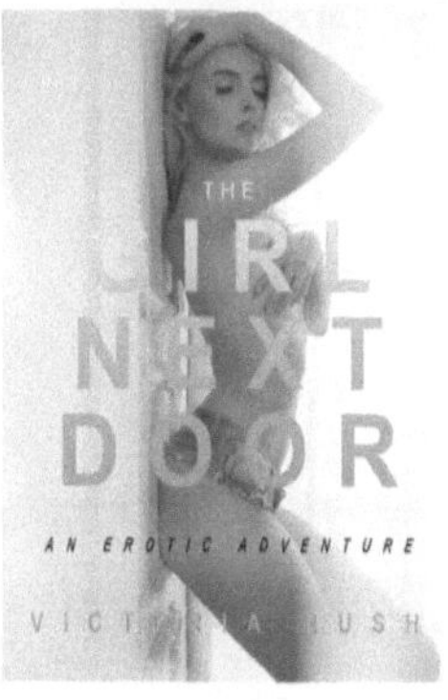

Spying on the neighbors just got a lot more interesting...